PUFFIN BOOKS

A Bad Case of Dinosaurs

Kenneth Oppel wrote his first children's book when he was a fifteen-year-old high school student in Victoria, British Columbia. Since then he has studied cinema and English literature at the University of Toronto, and written several other books for both children and young adults. He lives in Canada with his wife, Philippa.

Other books by Kenneth Oppel

A BAD CASE OF GHOSTS
A BAD CASE OF MAGIC
A BAD CASE OF ROBOTS

A Bad Case of Dinosaurs

Kenneth Oppel

Illustrated by
Peter Utton

PUFFIN BOOKS

To Philippa

PUFFIN BOOKS

Published by the Penguin Group
Penguin Books Ltd, 27 Wrights Lane, London w8 5tz, England
Penguin Books USA Inc., 375 Hudson Street, New York, New York 10014, USA
Penguin Books Australia Ltd, Ringwood, Victoria, Australia
Penguin Books Canada Ltd, 10 Alcorn Avenue, Toronto, Ontario, Canada m4v 3b2
Penguin Books (NZ) Ltd, 182–190 Wairau Road, Auckland 10, New Zealand

Penguin Books Ltd, Registered Offices: Harmondsworth, Middlesex, England

First published by Hamish Hamilton Ltd 1994
Published in Puffin Books 1995
1 3 5 7 9 10 8 6 4 2

Text copyright © Kenneth Oppel, 1994
Illustrations copyright © Peter Utton, 1994
All rights reserved

The moral right of the author and illustrator has been asserted

Filmset in 15pt Baskerville by Rowland Phototypesetting Ltd

Made and printed in Great Britain by Clays Ltd, St Ives plc

Chapter 1

GILES SETTLED BACK in the bathtub with a contented sigh.

He'd just managed to work up a thick bubbly foam on the water's surface, when the bathroom door suddenly flew open and Tina and Kevin Quark walked straight in, and stood at the edge of the tub, looking down at him expectantly. Giles could only stare back at them, speechless.

"Knocking," he managed to say. "Ever heard of it?"

"We have secured another commission," said Tina grandly.

"We've got a job," added Kevin.

"Kevin," said Tina with a weary sigh, "that's what I just said."

"Could have fooled me."

Giles slid lower down in the tub, the water lapping against his chin.

Life had seemed so simple before he'd met Tina and Kevin. Now that he'd been fully promoted to their genius business, it seemed he never had a moment's peace. Just last week, they'd been hired to deal with the Walsh's missing garden gnomes, and the Angelini's creaking hinges. Then there'd been a particularly nasty case involving a radio which only picked up country and western music. It didn't matter where the tuning needle was, or whether the radio was on or off, the same mournful voice and guitar strumming blared from the speakers.

3

Giles supposed he should feel grateful that business was going full blast. After all, he'd almost saved up enough for the remote-controlled airplane he'd had his eye on for months. But he couldn't help wishing things would slow down just a little.

"Here I am, just trying to enjoy a simple bath," he said to Tina and Kevin, "and in you come like the

Charge of the Valkyrie!"

"Charge of the *what*?" said Kevin.

"Giles is saying we just barged in," Tina explained.

"Well, I suppose we did," said Kevin good-naturedly. "Sorry about that, Giles."

"Oh no, not at all!" he said. "Look, just climb right in, both of you!"

"Thank you, Giles," said Tina, "but we're rather pressed for time. Maybe at some later date."

"It was a joke," said Giles, rolling his eyes. "So, what's this new job?"

"A Miss Frost telephoned," said Tina, taking a small notebook from her pocket. "She says there's a problem with her swimming pool."

"What kind of problem?"

"How much do you know about underwater life forms, Giles?"

"You know," said Kevin helpfully, "squiggly things with tentacles and suckers the size of—"

"In her swimming pool?" said Giles, glancing nervously at the bath water. "You must be joking!"

"All I know," said Tina calmly, "is that Miss Frost seems to think she has something strange living in her pool. I personally doubt very much that this is the case, but we'll need to make a full investigation tomorrow morning."

"Fine," said Giles. "Now if you'll both excuse me, I'm going to pull the plug."

Chapter 2

THE BIG DOOR swung slowly open.

"Mr Frost?" said Giles uncertainly.

"No," replied the man in the three-piece suit, "I'm Swift, Miss Frost's personal assistant. You must be the Quark geniuses. Miss Frost has been expecting you. Please come in."

It was like a museum inside. Giles looked around the grand hallway in amazement. There were Roman busts on columns, ancient tapestries and paintings hanging from the walls, ornate rugs covering the floor.

"An exquisite collection of Dutch

7

Old Masters," Tina commented, nodding at a row of paintings. "Miss Frost must be a woman of some distinction."

"Wow!" Kevin exclaimed. "Look at all this stuff! It must be worth a fortune!"

"It is," said the assistant, giving Kevin a disdainful look. "So please don't touch anything. Follow me."

As they passed the living room, Giles thought there was an oddly empty feel to the place. He could see now that there was a fine, dusty silt over all the antique furniture and beautiful ornaments. Old cobwebs trailed from the picture frames.

Swift led them up a swirling marble staircase, then down a long, dimly lit corridor which ended with a set of wide double doors.

8

"Miss Frost's office is through here," the assistant told them, turning the huge door knob. "Go in, please."

It was the biggest room Giles had ever seen.

Blinds covered all the windows, casting slices of dusty light into the room. A whole wall was filled with television monitors, scrolling numbers across their screens at a dizzying rate. At the far end of the room was a huge desk, with a long row of telephones on top.

And behind the desk sat an elegant, middle-aged woman. She was very pale, as if she hadn't seen the sun for quite some time. At the moment she was talking into one of the telephones.

"What do you mean, he won't sell?" she demanded in a steel-cold voice. "There's nothing that can't be bought!

Everything has it's price. Offer half a
million! That should do the trick!"

She slammed down the phone and
looked up fiercely at Giles, Kevin and
Tina.

"So," she said, "you're the Quark
geniuses."

"Well, they are," stammered Giles,
pointing to Tina and Kevin.

"What are you then?" asked Miss
Frost with a scowl.

"I'm Giles Barnes."

"Not a genius yourself, young man?"

"I'm afraid not, no," replied Giles awkwardly.

"Most regrettable."

At that moment, all the telephones on her desk went off like a bomb.

"Buy!" she barked into the first phone.

"Sell!" she yelled into the second.

"Tell her if she pulls out we'll sue!" she roared into a third.

Giles swallowed hard.

"Right, then," said Miss Frost calmly, "where were we?"

Tina cleared her throat, and opened her notebook.

"Miss Frost, I can see you're very busy, so we'll try to take as little of your time as possible. Perhaps you could tell us more about your swimming pool problem."

"It's obvious to me that something is living in it," Miss Frost said matter-of-factly. "I'm not talking about ducks or geese or swans. Twice this past week, I've seen some sort of strange creature break the surface of the water, float on top for a moment, then dive back down again."

"What did this creature look like?" Tina asked.

"I've only seen it at night from the window," Miss Frost replied, "so I didn't get a very good look. But it reminded me of a giant jellyfish, or a squid."

Kevin looked over at Giles and smiled weakly. Tina was busily taking notes.

"And there have been noises," Miss

Frost went on. "A kind of gurgling moan."

"A gurgling moan?" squeaked Kevin.

"Yes."

"Have you ever seen it swimming round in daylight?" Giles asked.

"It's not that simple," she replied. "It's a very large pool, and in very poor repair. I've simply been too busy to keep it up and – well, you'll see what I mean soon enough."

"What would you like us to do exactly?" Giles asked.

"I want a full investigation," said Miss Frost. "I want a comprehensive report. I want to know if what I've seen is truly some strange creature, or a figment of my imagination. And, of course," she added, raising a pale finger in the air, "I insist that you keep

this matter strictly secret. I don't want
any of this spread about, not even to
your parents. Rumours start so
quickly, and I wouldn't want people to
think I was –"

"A complete loony," Kevin said
helpfully. Then he looked down at his
feet, his face flushing bright red.

"You'll have to excuse my brother, Miss Frost," said Tina. "Sadly, he was not blessed with as large a brain as my own. In fact, in numerous tests I've performed on him, it seems he really only has a very tiny brain."

"I see," said Miss Frost. "So it turns out I've hired one genius for the price of three."

"I think you'll find my brain more than makes up for the others," said Tina with supreme confidence.

"I sincerely hope so," said Miss Frost. "Swift will show you to the pool now."

Outside Miss Frost's door, Swift waited for them, standing as still as a department store mannequin. They were led back downstairs, and outside onto a broad terrace surrounded on all sides by a ferociously overgrown garden.

"Here we are," said the assistant.

Giles frowned. "Um, where's the swimming pool?"

"Here we are," Swift said again, looking straight ahead, hands clasped behind his back.

"I don't understand," Kevin said.

Swift sighed, picked up a small stone and threw it into a ragged patch of greenery.

Plok!

"There's water underneath all that?" said Giles, incredulous.

"As Miss Frost indicated, it's in rather poor repair," said the assistant, and with that he turned and marched away.

All three of them stood there in stunned silence.

Giles walked cautiously to the edge of the concrete terrace for a better look. It was as if the entire garden had just grown right into the swimming pool. A thick carpet of green algae and lily pads covered the water, and strange-looking plants sprouted leafy tendrils across the surface.

"Look at all that glurp!" said Kevin.

"That's not a word, Kevin," Tina told him.

"I'd say glurp is a pretty good word for what we're looking at," Giles said.

A big, oily bubble bulged on the water's surface and burst with a thick popping sound.

"It's like a prehistoric swamp!" he exclaimed. "How are we supposed to see what's in the pool?"

Tina turned thoughtfully to her brother.

19

"Kevin, how would you feel about stripping down and just having a little paddle around?"

"Forget it!" Kevin exclaimed.

"No, I thought not," said Tina regretfully.

"You really think there's some weird creature in there?" Giles said.

"Of course not," said Tina confidently. "I'm sure there's a perfectly reasonable explanation for what Miss Frost saw."

Another big bubble popped the water's surface, and a gurgling moan welled up from the depths of the pool.

Giles looked nervously over at Kevin.

"Could have been the wind," Kevin said quickly.

"Well," said Tina, "there's only one way to find out. We'll have to go

underwater with the bathysphere!"

"The bathysphere?" Giles said to
Kevin.

"Don't even ask," Kevin replied
wearily.

Chapter 3

"IT LOOKS LIKE a washing machine!"
Giles exclaimed.

Tina sighed long-sufferingly.

"Giles, even the greatest inventors
are forced to work with the raw
materials at hand. In this instance, a
washing machine happened to be a
most suitable starting point."

"Mum was not pleased," panted
Kevin, who had single-handedly
pushed the huge contraption from
home. He was lying flat on his back on
Miss Frost's terrace, catching his
breath.

"We can't go underwater in this!" Giles said. "Look! There are still dials on top that say RINSE and SPIN CYCLE!"

"I don't think either of you fully appreciate the greatness of my latest invention," Tina said haughtily. "This bathysphere is capable of going underwater to great depths, while safely carrying three people inside. It will enable us to make a thorough aquatic examination of the pool."

Giles walked slowly around the bathysphere, taking a good look. Tina had certainly made a lot of alterations. At the rear was a huge propeller which looked suspiciously like the ceiling fan in the Quark's dining room. Four bicycle lights had been bolted to the front. On either side of the bathysphere was bolted a big oil drum.

They sounded hollow when Giles tapped them. Thick rubber hosing was wrapped all around the outside, and truck tyres were nailed to the base. It was certainly much larger than a regular washing machine. Giles peered through the round glass hatch. Still, it looked like a tight squeeze in there.

"I'm not sure about this," Giles said.

"It's perfectly safe, Giles," Tina said. "I've tested it extensively."

"That's what you said about the turbo toaster," Kevin reminded her. "Dad nearly lost an eye." He turned to Giles. "That toast came out of there like a rocket!"

"Fine," said Tina, "I'll go alone. All the more glory for me, making the first descent all by myself –"

"All right, all right," sighed Giles.

After all, she was a genius. "We're coming."

He helped Kevin to his feet and, together, they rolled the bathysphere off the deck and into the swampy water. It rode high on the surface, buoyed up by the rubber tyres and oil drums.

Tina opened the round glass hatch.

"Everyone in," she said.

It was a terrible crush. Giles thought the inside looked like pictures he'd seen of an airplane cockpit, with switches, gauges and buttons on all sides, and overhead, too. He found it all rather reassuring. Something with this many switches must work.

Tina clanged the hatch shut behind her and sat between Giles and Kevin at the controls.

"Beginning descent!" said Tina, pushing buttons and throwing levers.

The bathysphere was slowly sinking. Giles watched as the gurgling water crept higher and higher up the round glass window. Soon it was level with his face and he could see half below, and half above the water. He caught himself holding his breath as the bathysphere sank completely under the surface.

It had become very dark all of a sudden, and Tina flipped another switch. The bicycle lights came on, and the water glowed eerily all around them.

Giles could barely believe they were in a swimming pool.

It certainly didn't look like one.

It was another world, murky green and vast. There was no sign of any walls. Far below them, the pool bottom was covered in a layer of dirt and stones so that it looked like the ocean bed. Fat gas bubbles wobbled past them towards the surface. A school of rainbow-coloured fish flitted across their path.

"Hey, how'd they get in here?" Kevin asked.

"There must be another way into this pool," Tina said solemnly.

27

She swooped the bathysphere deeper along the bottom.

"Look at that!" said Giles, pointing.

Lying toppled along the bottom was a huge statue of Poseidon.

"It must have fallen in from the terrace," said Kevin. "Wow. It's like the lost continent of Atlantis down here!"

"Never mind that," said Tina, "I think I've found something interesting."

She played the lights on a long jagged crack in the pool floor near the statue. The crack was quite wide – about a metre, Giles guessed.

"There must be an underground river underneath," said Tina. "Or else all the water would have drained through that crack. Let's have a closer look, shall we?"

"Gork!" said Kevin suddenly.

"Sorry, I didn't quite get that, Kevin," Tina said.

"Thlurk!" Kevin managed to say.

Giles looked over to see Kevin pointing out the window with a trembling hand, his eyes huge.

"Th . . . th . . . there's something moving over there."

"Are you certain?" asked Tina.

Kevin nodded.

Tina jiggled a few switches and the beams of light swept round.

"I don't see anything," said Giles. "What did it look like Kevin?"

"Big. Big and flappy."

"Big and flappy," said Tina, shaking her head with a sigh. "Very scientific, Kevin, thank you."

"Big and flappy and kind of green."

"Ah, excellent," said Tina sarcastically.

Something struck suddenly against the bathysphere window.

Something big and flappy, and definitely green.

"That's it!" wailed Kevin. "That's what I saw!"

It was gone so quickly, Giles didn't even have time to focus on it.

"Let's surface!" said Kevin. "This isn't fun any more!"

"Certainly not!" said Tina. "Not when we've just made visual contact!"

"There it is again!" said Giles.

"Don't go too close," said Kevin, his voice quavering.

Tina fixed the creature with the spotlight. She sighed.

"So this is it, is it? Big and flappy and green."

It was a tattered tarpaulin, floating just off the bottom of the pool, its ratty edges undulating like tentacles.

"It looked so much bigger when I saw it," Kevin said sheepishly.

"This must be Miss Frost's creature," said Giles with relief.

"Yes," said Tina wisely. "A gas bubble must lift the tarpaulin up through the water. At the top, all the

gas escapes, and it sinks back down to
the bottom. It could keep going up and
down like that forever."

"Well," said Kevin, who'd cheered
up considerably, "that's another case
cracked by the Quark genius
business." He nudged Giles. "See, it
wasn't worth getting so frightened
about, was it?"

Something pushed up against the
bathysphere window, blotting out the
light.

32

"Gork!" said Kevin again.

Giles knew exactly what he meant this time.

This wasn't a tarpaulin.

This was something else.

This something had a purple, wedge-shaped head with green-rimmed eyes, and a long, narrow mouth lined with two sharp mountain ranges of teeth!

Chapter 4

MISS FROST LOOKED up as they burst into her office.

"You've got something all right!" Kevin blurted out, skidding across the floor.

"A creature!" said Giles. "There is definitely a strange creature living in your pool!"

"I see," Miss Frost replied calmly. "You're quite certain of that, are you?"

"Certain?" said Kevin. "You should have seen the teeth on that thing!"

"Thank you, Kevin," said Tina

34

firmly, "that will be quite enough. Miss Frost, I'm pleased to report that I have made visual contact with the creature in question, and have managed to make an identification."

"Go on," she said.

Giles had never seen anyone take such extraordinary news so calmly.

"Unless I'm mistaken," Tina began, "and I so rarely am, the creature is actually a very rare species of Hydrosaurus."

"Are you telling me I have a dinosaur living in my pool?"

"Yes I am, Miss Frost."

"How did it get there?"

"Through a crack in the bottom," said Giles. "It must swim in from some underground river. After we saw it, it darted back down through the crack."

A telephone rang. Miss Frost picked

it up, said, "Not now," and hung up.

She looked back at the three of them and smiled. "Excellent. A splendid job."

"Well, I think that about wraps things up here," said Kevin eagerly. "It's been a real pleasure, Miss Frost. We'll send you our bill and –"

"No, no," said Miss Frost. "You're not finished yet."

"We're not?" said Giles.

"I wonder how much a dinosaur is worth?" Miss Frost said quietly, looking at the flashing wall of television screens. "It's one of a kind. I'd be the only person in the world to have one."

She looked sternly at the three of them.

"I want you to catch it for me."

"Catch it?" exclaimed Kevin.

"Miss Frost," said Giles, "catching dinosaurs really isn't the kind of thing we do."

"It's not at all," agreed Kevin. "I mean, the last time we caught dinosaurs was –"

"I want that Hydrosaurus," said Miss Frost in her steely voice.

"I'm sure we could trap it for you," said Tina confidently.

Giles stared at her in amazement.

"But –" he began to say.

"But –" Kevin began to say.

"Good!" said Miss Frost. "That's the kind of attitude I like in my business."

She opened a drawer and took out the thickest cheque book Giles had ever seen.

"And rest assured," she said, "I'll

make it very worth your while."

"I can't believe we're actually trying to catch a dinosaur," said Giles nervously.

"It's a scientific breakthrough," said Tina grandly. "Think of it, Giles. Before now, all we've had to go on are dinosaur bones. But now we've discovered a living specimen! It might be millions of years old! Or this particular species might never have died out at all! It's absolutely essential we catch it!"

"Besides," added Kevin, "did you see the size of Miss Frost's cheque book? We're going to be rich!"

They'd been waiting in the bathysphere for a long time now, hovering at the bottom of the pool near the large crack. But so far there'd been no sign of the Hydrosaurus.

"I don't understand why the dinosaur keeps coming back here anyway," said Giles.

"After we catch it," said Tina, flipping some switches, "and I have time to study it properly, perhaps I'll have an answer to that question."

"I just hope this plan of yours works," said Giles dubiously.

All at once the dinosaur flashed up through the crack and circled gracefully through the water. For the first time, Giles got a good look at it. Its skin was a deep purple, with brilliant streaks of green. Its body was

quite slender, with four leathery fins
jutting out from its sides. It had a very
long, very thin neck, which ended with
its small wedge-shaped head.

"Look at it move!" said Giles in
awe. "It's so fast!"

"Here we go!" said Tina excitedly. She edged the bathysphere forward until it nudged against the huge statue of Poseidon. The propeller whirred loudly, and the whole vessel began to shudder.

"The statue's too big!" shouted Giles.

"It won't budge!" cried Kevin.

"We have the power!" said Tina through gritted teeth.

The propeller's whining increased in pitch, and the bathysphere was shaking so violently Giles thought it would burst apart at any moment. But slowly the statue of Poseidon began to scrape across the pool floor towards the long crack.

"It's working!" said Tina.

A second Hydrosaurus suddenly darted up through the opening, this one was slightly smaller, with a pink underbelly. The two dinosaurs rolled through the water playfully together.

"Look!" gasped Giles. "We've got two now!"

"We've got a bad case of

dinosaurs!" said Kevin.

Tina threw another lever and the bathysphere pushed ahead some more, and in a few seconds, the statue rolled into place over the crack, blocking the opening completely.

"Miss Frost," Tina said with satisfaction, "is now the proud owner of two dinosaurs."

Chapter 5

GILES WRINKLED HIS nose as he plunged his hand into the bucket, grabbed another fish and threw it into the pool. One of the dinosaurs snapped it up before it even hit water.

"They sure do eat a lot," said Kevin, lobbing a cod tail to the other Hydrosaurus.

"Good job, you two," said Tina, "keep it up." She was stretched out on a lawn chair at the poolside, a micro cassette recorder in one hand, a glass of iced tea in the other. Every so often, she would lift the cassette recorder to her face, speak into it, then smile and shake her head with a small chuckle, as if what she'd just said was the most amusing and remarkable thing she'd ever heard.

Giles rolled his eyes in disgust.

"I don't suppose you want to take a turn feeding them?" he asked.

"No need to be sarcastic, Giles," Tina replied. "Anyone can see I'm extremely busy making scientific notes on these specimens."

"Right," Giles grumbled.

Every day after school, for the past week, he and Kevin had made the trip to the local fish shop to buy pounds and pounds of raw fish for the Hydrosaurs. The bus driver refused to let them on with their stinking buckets of dinosaur food, so they had to lug them all the way to Miss Frost's house by foot. People on the street would sniff, then stop, then sniff again, then stare as they passed by. It was not pleasant.

"This is going to make headlines," Tina said contentedly. "'Local geniuses discover dinosaurs.' Or maybe, 'Breakthrough of century made by local genius.' Or what about 'Tina Quark wins Nobel Prize'? It's been far too long since I was on the cover of a newspaper."

"At least you're not the one who goes home smelling like a barnacle every day," Giles told her.

"You've got nothing to complain about, Giles," Tina said. "Miss Frost is paying us all very generously to tend to the dinosaurs. A few more days and you'll have enough for that remote controlled airplane you've wanted for so long. Don't you want to be rich?"

Giles sighed.

He supposed he did want to be rich. After all, who didn't? And he definitely wanted that airplane. Yesterday he'd passed the shop window where it was displayed. He was always a little afraid that the next time, it would be gone.

Soon, though, he'd be able to walk right into the store, put his money down on the counter, and take the airplane home himself.

But he felt bristly and out of sorts. And it wasn't just because he had to heft buckets of smelly fish around every day. He looked at the two Hydrosaurs in the pool.

"I don't think they're very happy, trapped like this," he told Tina.

"Don't be ridiculous, Giles," said. Tina. "They have brains the size of grape seeds. Would you feel sorry for a goldfish in a bowl? I think not. These creatures probably don't even realize they're trapped!"

But Giles wasn't so sure. After they'd rolled the statue of Poseidon over the crack, the two Hydrosaurs had prodded at it with their heads, and darted to and fro in confusion. And a ghostly moaning had drifted through the water. It was the most mournful thing Giles had ever heard.

And Giles thought they looked a little listless sometimes, floating near the surface, with their wedge-shaped heads peering out at them. Other times, they definitely seemed restless, churning the swampy water into a froth as they tore around the perimeter of the pool, faster and faster, as if they were desperate to escape.

"How do you know they're so stupid?" Giles asked.

"Everyone knows the dinosaurs weren't terribly bright," Tina replied wisely. "All these creatures can do is swim and eat. They're savage beasts. They're eating machines."

"I wonder what Miss Frost is going

to do with them?" Giles wondered aloud.

It wasn't as if she'd taken any real interest in the dinosaurs. She hadn't even come down to the poolside to have a close look. A few times, Giles had turned to see her watching from her office window, but, once spotted, she always quickly disappeared from sight. What a strange person she was, Giles thought, working all alone in that vast house, with only her creepy personal assistant, Swift, for company!

"I want to get a picture of the dinosaurs," said Kevin, taking an instamatic camera from his satchel. "Giles, can you stand by the edge, holding a fish?"

"Do I have to?"

"Yeah. It'll be a great photo."

Giles faced Kevin, holding a fish

head as far away from his body as
possible.

"A little further back, Giles. You're
not in the picture."

He took another step back.

"A little more! Plenty of room!"

Another few steps.

"Um, Giles . . ." he heard Kevin
say suddenly.

The next thing he knew, he was
deep in the pool, swampy water

shooting up his nostrils. Spluttering, he fought to get back to the surface, but his clothing was sodden, and it was dragging him down. He'd never felt more terrified in his life. His head popped up for a moment, and he managed to suck in a breath of air before sinking under again.

I'm a goner! he thought in pure panic. I'm about to get eaten by dinosaurs!

Opening his eyes, he made out a blurry purple shape swirling around him, and then felt it brush past him. This is it, he thought, gritting his teeth. Here it comes. He felt the dinosaur nudge its head against his backside, and then push hard. Giles was propelled up and out of the water, as if he were in an ejector seat! He sailed through the air, and landed at the edge of the pool, streaming

water, still spluttering.

"Wow!" gasped Kevin.

"Extraordinary!" said Tina, who had taken her glass of iced tea and was standing at the poolside with Kevin.

"Am I ever sorry, Giles!" said Kevin worriedly, slapping him on the back. "I had no idea you were so close to the edge! I was about to dive in and save you!"

"You most certainly were not, Kevin," said Tina witheringly.

"Well, I was planning on doing something!" Kevin said. "Are you OK, Giles?"

Giles nodded. He still felt a little shaky. He could see the dinosaur's head poking above the water, watching him with its bright eyes.

"It didn't eat me!" he stammered. "It lifted me out!"

He'd heard all sorts of stories about shipwrecked sailors being saved from drowning by dolphins. He'd just been saved by a Hydrosaurus!

"They must be smarter than you think, Tina," Kevin told his sister.

"And friendlier," Giles said.

"And much cuddlier than I first thought," added Kevin, waving at the dinosaur in the pool.

Tina frowned, then stalked back to
her lawn chair and started muttering
into her cassette recorder.

Chapter 6

GILES LOOKED AT the remote-controlled airplane in the shop window.

"It's a beauty all right," Kevin said.

Giles crinkled the money in his pocket. He'd waited a long time for this airplane, and now, thanks to their dinosaur job, he could finally buy it. He knew every detail of the airplane by now, and had often daydreamed about taking it on its first flight in the big field near his house.

"It's great being rich, isn't it?" said Kevin cheerfully. "Now I can buy a radio to replace the one Tina blew up last month. Those dinosaurs are the best thing that's ever happened to the genius business!"

Giles jammed his hands into his pockets and turned away from the window.

"Aren't you going to buy it?" Kevin asked in confusion.

"We've got to set them free," Giles said.

"What? The dinosaurs?"

"It's not fair to keep them trapped in that pool," said Giles. "And all because Miss Frost wants to own the only dinosaurs in the world! It's just like all those other beautiful things in her house, collecting dust! It's just greedy!"

How could he possibly buy the airplane with the money Miss Frost

61

had given him? He knew he'd feel too guilty.

"Do you really think they mind staying in the pool?" Kevin asked with a frown.

"How would you like to be all boxed up?"

"Tina was thinking about it once," Kevin replied thoughtfully, "but I managed to talk her out of it. You're right, Giles, I don't think it would be very nice at all."

"They're not eating as much as they used to, either," Giles said. "They're definitely unhappy. We should let them loose."

Kevin shook his head uncertainly.

"Tina won't like it," he said. "Do you know what she's doing right now? She's at home, dictating her memoirs! Once I passed her door and heard her

practising some kind of acceptance
speech. She kept saying things like
'Thank you for this great honour' and
'I knew it was only a matter of time
before my great genius was recognized
by the international community.' She's
counting on these dinosaurs, Giles. She
thinks they're going to make her world
famous!"

"We'll have to do it without telling
her."

"But what about Miss Frost? She's not going to let us set them free. She owns the dinosaurs! And you've heard the way she talks to people on the telephone! She's tough, Giles. She's downright scary! There's no way we'll ever convince her!"

"There's only one way," said Giles. "We've got to make her a deal."

Swift opened the door, blinked, and stared in amazement.

On the doorstep stook Giles and Kevin, both dressed in large, dark suits and ties borrowed from Mr Barnes's closet. Kevin wore sunglasses and a scowl. His hair was slicked back with half a bottle of hair gel, and both his arms were folded menacingly across his chest. Giles held a briefcase in one hand.

"We're here to see Miss Frost," he said.

Without waiting for a reply, he and Kevin walked quickly through the door and headed for the swirling marble staircase.

"Wait! You can't just march in

here!" Swift objected, running to block their way. "Miss Frost is far too busy to be bothered by unannounced visitors."

"Move aside, sir," said Kevin in a very deep, very serious voice. "We don't want anyone getting hurt."

Swift stepped back without hesitation. Giles was impressed.

They made their way quickly up the stairs. Kevin, practically blind in his sunglasses, had to feel his way along the bannister to avoid tripping.

Miss Frost was on the telephone when they barged into her office.

"I'll make him an offer he can't refuse!" she growled. Snatching up another phone she said, "Tell him he'd better sell now, or he'll be eating potatoes for the rest of his life!"

Giles gulped.

Maybe this wasn't such a good idea after all. But it was too late now. Miss Frost had caught sight of them and was frowning curiously.

"I'll call you back in a few minutes," she said into the phone.

Giles took a deep breath, handed his

briefcase to Kevin, and strode up to the huge desk.

"Miss Frost," he said, trying to sound firm and professional, "I have a deal for you."

"Is that Giles Barnes?"

"That's correct."

"And who is this with you?"

"That's my personal assistant."

"How did you get his hair to do that?"

"Never mind that right now, Miss Frost."

"Why is he wearing sunglasses?"

"To look menacing," Kevin said helpfully.

Miss Frost glanced at her day planner.

"I don't believe we have an appointment pencilled in for today," she said.

"No, we don't," said Giles brusquely. "But this simply couldn't wait."

"Oh?"

"I want to buy those dinosaurs, Miss Frost, and I'm prepared to make you a cash offer right now."

Giles thought there was a sparkle of admiration in her eyes.

"Go on," she said.

Giles suddenly drew a blank. He simply didn't know what to say next. Instead he snapped his fingers. Kevin stepped forward obediently and helped him off with his jacket, draping it over his arm. Giles cleared his throat and adjusted his tie knot. He had no idea what he was doing, but it all seemed incredibly professional. For good measure he snapped his fingers again and Kevin stepped forward with the

jacket and helped Giles back into it.

He felt much better now.

"Let me be candid, Miss Frost. Allow me to get straight to the heart of the matter. I'm not a man to mince words. Speaking as one businessperson to another, I think we can hammer out a deal which is mutually beneficial."

71

He hadn't the slightest idea where all these words were coming from, but they poured into his mind thick and fast.

"I think you'll find my offer speaks for itself."

He snapped his fingers again and Kevin brought over the briefcase and set it on Miss Frost's desk. Giles gave a curt nod and Kevin opened the clasps and flipped up the top. Inside was a small, rumpled stack of banknotes, held together by an elastic band. Scattered loose across the bottom of the briefcase was an assortment of coins.

Miss Frost carefully counted the money. Giles looked over at Kevin and smiled weakly. Would it be enough? He didn't think it looked nearly as impressive as it had earlier in his bedroom. But it was all the money he'd saved up for the remote controlled airplane, plus some of Kevin's savings from the genius business.

"You realize, of course," said Miss Frost, "that these dinosaurs are worth over a million times the amount you have here."

Giles instantly felt ridiculous.

"Really?"

"I'm afraid so, yes."

"Well," said Giles, "this is all I've got."

Miss Frost looked at him curiously. "And you're willing to spend all of it on the dinosaurs?"

Giles nodded firmly.

"I see. And what were you planning to do with them?"

"Set them free."

Miss Frost stared in disbelief. "But why?"

Giles faltered. Nothing he could say would convince her; to her the dinosaurs were already huge numbers on one of her television screens, not animals at all. But suddenly he had an idea.

"Maybe you should come down and have a look," he suggested. "You've never really seen them up close."

"No time," she said brusquely.

"It won't take very long. Really.".

"You'd be one of the only people on the planet to see a real live dinosaur!" Kevin added from behind his sunglasses.

Miss Frost appeared to consider this, then glanced quickly around the room at the flashing television monitors. "All right. I'll give you fifteen minutes," she said. She moved slowly from her desk, eyes fixed warily on the silent phones, as if afraid that too sudden a movement would trigger an explosion of ringing. "Better make it ten minutes," she decided.

On the stairs, the three of them ran into Swift, lugging up a huge stack of computer printouts. When he caught sight of Miss Frost, he jumped as if he'd seen a ghost, scattering sheafs of paper across the steps.

"Miss Frost?" he said in amazement. "Is – is that you?"

"Of course it's me," she said impatiently.

"But what are you – why aren't – you aren't in your office!"

"Yes, I realize it's been quite a while since I've left my office, Swift, but I want to have a quick look at these dinosaurs."

"You're not going down in that tin-can contraption of theirs, surely!"

"That is my intention, Swift, yes."

From upstairs came the insistent bleating of one telephone, then two, then three. Miss Frost froze, listening anxiously.

Oh no, thought Giles. She's not going to come after all.

"Deal with it, Swift," said Miss Frost impulsively. "Better yet, let them

ring. They'll call back if it's important.
I want to see these dinosaurs."

Swift just stared as Miss Frost
walked past him, down the stairs
towards the pool.

Chapter 7

"THEY'RE BEAUTIFUL!" exclaimed Miss Frost, peering at the dinosaurs through the bathysphere's glass hatch. "Look at them move!"

Giles guided the bathysphere smoothly down to the bottom of the pool. He'd watched Tina enough times to know how to handle the controls. The two Hydrosaurs swooped gracefully through the water around them.

"But why did they come in the first place?" Miss Frost asked.

Giles shook his head. "Tina thought that maybe they got lost on their way to the ocean."

In the distance, in the far corner of the pool, Giles made out a small mound of stones which he'd never noticed before.

"What's that?" he said, steering the bathysphere over.

All at once the two dinosaurs cut in front of him, blocking his way. Again and again, they streaked anxiously past the hatch, making a low, gurgling moan.

"They don't want you to go any closer!" Kevin said.

"I wonder why?" said Miss Frost.

Giles squinted at the strange mound and caught a glimpse of something white nestled amongst the rocks.

Suddenly everything made sense.

"Look! It's an egg!" he shouted. "That's why they came here. To make a nest. It's the perfect place for it, too. Safe and quiet!"

As they all watched, the egg began to shudder slightly.

"It's hatching!" said Kevin.

The two Hydrosaurs swam in close and swirled around the egg, so that Giles couldn't see what was going on very well. But after a few minutes, he managed to catch a glimpse of a small, bright red, wedge-shaped head, peeping out from the top of the cracked egg.

"Set them free," said Miss Frost suddenly.

Giles looked over at her in surprise, a smile breaking out on his face.

"You mean it?"

She nodded. "I've been trapped up

in that office of mine for years, waiting
for phones to ring and monitors to
flicker. It's ridiculous. And it's
nobody's fault but my own. But these
animals don't have much say in the
matter, do they. It's not right to keep
them trapped in my pool – or anyone
else's if it comes to that. So let's set
them free."

Giles turned the bathysphere round
and pushed up against the huge statue

of Poseidon. He opened the throttle to full, and the propeller whirred furiously. Gradually the statue scraped across the pool floor until the crack was completely uncovered.

The dinosaurs didn't waste a second.

The first Hydrosaurus shot down through the opening like a flash of purple lightning. Then the red, baby Hydrosaurus swam a little clumsily

towards the crack, nudged along by
the smaller dinosaur. After the baby
wobbled down out of sight, the last
Hydrosaurus circled magnificently
around the bathysphere once, then
darted into the fissure and was gone.

Tina stood by the edge of the pool, eyes fixed on the still, swamp-like surface of the water.

"I'm trying to remain calm," she said.

"That's good," said Kevin nervously. "Breathe deeply."

"I am breathing deeply, Kevin. I am breathing as deeply as I know how. If I breathe any deeper I am going to blow up like a balloon and POP!"

Kevin jumped.

Tina turned a forlorn face to Giles. "Do you have any idea what you've done?"

"I think I'm about to find out," Giles replied.

"You've destroyed my career, Giles. I'm finished. Ruined. Washed up. I spent the best days of my life studying those two dinosaurs. I was ready to make scientific history! They were the only two living dinosaurs ever seen by mankind."

"Three," Kevin reminded her good-naturedly. "Don't forget the baby Hydrosaurus."

"Thank you, Kevin," said Tina through clenched teeth. "Of course, I didn't get the chance to see the baby dinosaur, thanks to you both! Did you know I'd been invited to speak at the university? Did you know I'd practically finished my memoirs? 'Tina Quark: A Brilliant Life.' It would have been a bestseller."

"Look on the bright side," said Kevin. "We've got another job for the genius business out of it. Miss Frost has hired us to clean up the pool and garden. It's going to be a very big job for us."

Tina shook her head dejectedly. "From award-winning scientist to yard maintenance," said Tina. "This is a sad day indeed. I'm completely at a loss."

"I'm not," said Giles, stretching his arms above his head with a yawn. "I know exactly what I'm going to do. I'm going to go home and have a nice, relaxing bath. And, if it's all the same to you, I'd like to have it *alone* this time."

Also in Young Puffin

The Village Dinosaur

Phyllis Arkle

"What's going on?"
"Something exciting!"
"Where?"
"Down at the old quarry."

It isn't every small boy who finds a living
dinosaur buried in a quarry, just as it
isn't every dinosaur that discovers Roman
remains and stops train smashes. Never
have so many exciting and improbable
things happened in one quiet village!